TOM PALMER

TAKE TO THE SKIES

WINGS: SPITFIRE

WITH ILLUSTRATIONS BY
DAVID SHEPHARD

Barrington Stoke

First published in 2016 in Great Britain by
Barrington Stoke Ltd
18 Walker Street, Edinburgh, EH3 7LP

www.barringtonstoke.co.uk

Text © 2016 Tom Palmer
Illustrations © 2016 David Shephard

A CIP catalogue record for this book is available
from the British Library upon request

ISBN: 978-1-78112-536-6

Printed in China by Leo

For Tom Nokes

ONE

Greg was inside the centre circle when it happened.

"Play the ball, Greg," he heard one of the coaches shout. "And get back into your goal. If you cross that half way line again I'll kick you off the pitch. In fact, I might kick you out of the summer school too if you're not careful."

But Greg didn't listen. He was intent on dribbling the ball forward, then playing a killer pass to one of his team's forwards. And the players on the other team were still backing off.

'Being a keeper is rubbish,' he thought. 'Things only happen to you. You never make them happen yourself.' But Greg would make things happen. And then, as soon as this game was over, he'd chuck his goalie gloves away for good.

And Greg pushed on, nudging the ball forward. As he did so, he heard a buzzing, humming sound, as if an old plane was flying above him. He glanced up at the sky. The dazzle from the sun blinded him.

And – in that second of lost focus – two of the opposition players rushed him fierce and fast.

No words.

No warning.

It was a pincer movement by the two sisters who'd been bothering him all game. Maddie and Jess.

Greg panicked.

And his panic made him retreat back to his goal, leaving the ball out on the pitch. That meant Maddie and Jess had it without a defender in sight.

Disaster.

Jatinder – the boy Greg had got to know best this week – was the only one of Greg's team-mates to react, but he was in the wrong half of the pitch.

As Greg scrambled back to his goal, he glanced over his shoulder, half expecting one of the sisters to loft the ball over him and into the net.

But the older one, Maddie, was still running with the ball as her sister moved off wide, yelling for the pass.

Greg could hear the coaches shouting at him again as he got back into the edge of his penalty area. They were furious.

So he chose that moment to turn round and face down the girls.

"Pass," he heard Jess shout. "Pass it to me!"

But Greg could see Maddie laughing as she bore down on the goal.

'She knows they'll score,' he said to himself. 'It's two against one. I don't stand a chance.'

Greg backed into his goal mouth some more, then stood tall as Maddie came at him. There was no way he could deal with it if she passed now.

"Paaaaassssss," Jess yelled again. She was standing in miles of clear space in front of the open goal.

Maddie shaped her body to pass. Greg glanced from sister to sister, and he knew his situation was hopeless.

But then – from nowhere – Jatinder arrived. He slid into the path of the pass, and his kick pushed the ball out of play as soon as it left Maddie's feet.

Greg found himself on his bum.

And from there he watched Jess bawl at Maddie for hogging the ball. "You are SO selfish!" she screamed. Maddie's reply was drowned out by the coach's yells about Greg being out of position – again. The coach told him to get himself off the pitch.

Greg closed his eyes. Everyone was angry about something. And he felt like the angriest of them all.

What had possessed him to sign up as a goalkeeper? He was an idiot.

Never again. Playing in goal was a nightmare. It was either full-on stress or standing around with nothing to do. It got you into trouble.

And Greg knew that a shed-load of trouble was heading his way right now.

TWO

Greg went straight to the dressing room after the match and stayed there. He sat on a bench with his back to the door, his bare feet on the cold tiles and his focus all on his phone screen. FightClub. He'd been thinking about how to reach the next level during the quiet bits of the match earlier.

But as he opened the game he could smell petrol. A dense, oily smell of fuel burning, or something like that. And there was the drone of an engine overhead again. He ignored it all and sank back into the world of FightClub.

Next, a voice.

"Greg. That coach is on his way. He's looking for you."

"Thanks, Jatinder," Greg said.

Jatinder was a good footballer and Greg was glad that the two of them were staying at Steve and Esther's house and not in the dorms at the football school. Steve and Esther lived in a big old house near the summer school. They were brilliant at looking after the kids who stayed there.

But Greg couldn't look up to check on Jatinder. Not now. He was deep in the game and he needed to win this level. He played on.

Then his phone was gone from his hand.

"What!" Greg stood up, ready to face down this latest challenge. "Jatinder. That's not funny ..."

But it wasn't Jatinder. Greg was face to football shirt with Hafeez, the coach Jatinder had been talking about. Greg glanced up and saw that Hafeez was frowning under his dark mop of hair.

"No devices at summer school," Hafeez said. "I've told you a dozen times."

"OK," Greg mumbled. "Sorry."

"No devices. No missing team meetings. No keepers coming up to the half way line. How many rules do I have to make to find one that you won't break, Greg?"

"There must be one," Greg joked.

Hafeez fixed him with a steady gaze. He didn't laugh. Or even smile.

"Sorry, Hafeez," Greg tried again. "I just ..."

Hafeez stepped back and sighed, more with disappointment than anger. "You just what?" he said.

The look on his coach's face made Greg feel like telling the truth. "I just don't like being in goal. It gets so boring."

"You what?" Hafeez said. "Are you kidding me? You signed up for summer school as a keeper. That's the reason you were offered a place."

"I know," Greg said. "But I've changed my mind. It's not for me."

"I didn't have you down as a quitter," Hafeez said. And then, after a pause, he said, "I thought you showed some talent as a keeper. You know your angles, for a start."

Greg knew Hafeez was right, but it wasn't enough. "Well, I am a quitter," he mumbled. "That's me."

Hafeez shook his head, unimpressed. "And why aren't you at the team meeting? We've all been waiting for you."

"I lost track of the time playing this," Greg said, and he tried to look Hafeez in the eye. "Meetings are boring. Talking is boring. Goalkeeping is boring. I like this game."

Silence.

Greg had that feeling you get when adults go quiet because they want you to work out what you've done wrong before they tell you off. His parents and teachers confronted him with that silence a lot.

Greg swallowed, trying not to go red.

"You've got a decision to make," the football coach said. "Two, in fact."

"OK?" Greg said. He tried to swallow again, but he couldn't. His throat felt too dry.

He liked Hafeez. He was strong and skilful and nothing fazed him. Greg didn't want to disappoint him any more than he already had.

"One. In goal or not in goal?"

"Not in goal," Greg said.

"I see," Hafeez said. "And two. Learning or not learning?"

"Learning," Greg said. He knew that this was the answer Hafeez wanted to hear.

"Better." Hafeez nodded again. "Learning it is then. I'm going to set you some homework."

"What?" Greg's voice came out high-pitched. "You don't get homework at football school."

"No, most people don't," Hafeez agreed. "But you do. And if you don't do it, I'll be talking to your mum – even if she is visiting your grandma in Poland. OK?"

Greg had no choice. "OK," he said. "What is it?"

"Go and look at the old airfield with Steve."

Greg was confused. "Airfield? Steve?"

"Steve whose house you're staying at," Hafeez said. "Trenchard House is next to an old airfield."

"But what's that got to do with me?"

"History," Hafeez said. "It's a place where you can learn some history. Ask Steve to tell you about the young men who flew from there – the stuff they did in their lives, the choices they made, were proper tough."

"What young men?" Greg asked. He still didn't get it.

"Pilots," Hafeez said. "Spitfire pilots, some of them not that much older than you, flew from the old airfield."

THREE

Greg was hiding from Steve, sitting on the step outside Trenchard House, playing FightClub on his phone. He'd forgotten about Spitfires and everything Hafeez had talked about. His mind was on his game.

It was a warm evening and Greg could smell a heavy scent coming off the trees. Or maybe it was something else. He couldn't pin it down, but it felt like there was always a whiff of petrol. Something like that.

Greg had decided that Steve and Esther's home was funny. Not "funny ha ha". Just funny. Odd. Weird. The strange droning noises and the faint stink of fuel didn't feel right. Maybe it was that airfield near by that Hafeez had talked about. Or maybe it was the house itself. Greg just knew that there was something odd about the place, something that made him uneasy and restless.

Soon Greg got frustrated that he kept failing to move up a level on FightClub. He thought about downloading another game, but there was no Wi-Fi here. He stared out into the thick woods around the house, exasperated.

A man's voice interrupted his thoughts. It was Steve.

"So here you are," Steve said. "I had a text from Hafeez. Says he set you some homework."

"Yeah?" Greg's heart dropped. He'd hoped Hafeez had been joking about the homework. He wanted to pretend that he knew nothing about it. But it always seemed better just to tell the truth, no matter what. He was rubbish at lying.

"What's the homework then?" Steve pressed.

Greg sighed, then put his phone in his pocket.

"My homework is for you to show me the airfield," he admitted. "Teach me about what the Spitfire pilots did. Something like that."

Steve nodded and, for all he tried to keep his face stern, Greg saw his eyes light up.

Greg followed Steve away from the house, towards the edge of a wood. A mass of dark trees spread out into the distance. To Greg's left and right was a huge flat area overgrown with bushes and grass. What few buildings there were looked to be falling down, their brick walls crumbling and their roofs caved in. Some of the buildings were as big as a sports hall. Bigger.

"These buildings were hangars," Steve said. "But the RAF hid most of the planes among the trees. The new RAF base is over on the other side of the woods, now," he went on. "But this is where the original airfield was. This open area under the grass, can you see?" Steve bent down to touch the crumbled concrete at his feet. "It's a runway. It ran for 500 metres up there."

Greg gazed across the open land. There was mist hanging heavy over the trees, then dipping down to ground level, revealing rays of evening sun that appeared and disappeared with the mist.

"What about those buildings?" Greg asked. "The little ones?"

"Nissen Huts," Steve told him. "That's where some of the pilots slept. Some of them slept in our house too. They had 20 pilots in each hut. Can you imagine?"

Greg shook his head. "This was really an airport?" he asked.

"An airfield," Steve said. "During the war – both wars. Spitfires flew from here in the Second World War. Some of the best pilots were from Poland, in fact."

As Steve spoke, Greg smelled a sudden sharp whiff of petrol and screwed up his face. Then, again, he heard the faint sound of a plane flying overhead.

"So why isn't it an airfield now?" he asked.

"No war ... no need," Steve said. "The government wanted to sell it. We bought the house a while back."

Then Greg glimpsed the rounded wings of something, maybe an old fighter plane among the trees. And sparks around it. He rubbed his eyes and shivered.

"What's that?" he asked.

"Where?"

Greg pointed into the woods, but the wings had vanished.

"Nothing," he said. "I thought I saw an old plane."

Steve looked hard at Greg for a second – did he believe him? – then he shrugged.

"Can we go back?" Greg asked. He was shivering again as if a cold wind had moved in.

"Yes," Steve said, "but when we get back, I don't want you playing on that phone of yours. Hafeez told me you were on it all day."

And with that, the mood of trust between them snapped. Greg scowled and turned away, but after a moment he realised he had no option but to follow Steve as he walked back to Trenchard House.

Inside, Greg was raging. He wanted to play FightClub. He'd done his homework, hadn't he?

But FightClub wasn't going to happen. The heat of Greg's anger cooled as he heard that noise again. The quiet, grumbling roar of a machine idling before it moved off. It filled Greg with a sense of unease – a sense that things weren't normal.

FOUR

By six that evening Greg was bored. His legs
felt twitchy, like he needed to go for a run, do
some speed drills, play 90 minutes of football.
But not in goal. Perhaps he could go out on the
old airfield for a kickabout with Jatinder.

Anything would be better than this. He
felt empty inside. Life without FightClub was
unbearable.

Esther and Steve were in the kitchen
washing up the dinner dishes. Greg could hear
the clink of cutlery on plates and the murmur
of their quiet voices.

"Can we watch *The Simpsons*, please?" Greg called out. Jatinder looked up from the book he was reading, which had an old photo of a pilot on the front.

Esther leaned round the doorframe. "I'm sorry, Greg," she said. "You and Steve agreed no more screen time today."

Greg felt a flash of fury.

"So what I am supposed to do?" he snapped. "I'm so bored."

Esther didn't reply as Steve came past her and into the room. He opened a drawer and began to rummage in it.

Greg stared at the table. Should he just go to bed? The longer he spent asleep the sooner this would be over. But it was only 6.15 p.m.

"Look." Steve came over and sat down beside Greg. He had a small box in his hands.

"What is it?" Greg asked. Steve handed it to him and he turned it over to look at the plane on the front.

"An Airfix kit," Steve said. "This one's a Spitfire."

"One of those plastic kits you glue together?"

"Yes," Steve said. "If you're bored, shall we do it together?"

Greg shrugged. It didn't look brilliant, but it was better than nothing. "OK," he said.

Steve removed a little clear bag of kit from the box. Two small grey plastic frames with the parts of a plane attached. Some paints and stickers.

"Shall we make it?" he asked. "Then you can paint it."

Steve sat down next to Greg and worked patiently on the plane with him. Steve did the tricky bits, those fiddly pieces where Greg's fingers just got all stuck with glue. But Steve let Greg put the pilot in his seat and fix the propeller onto the nose of the plane. Then he handed him the wings to attach.

As they worked, Steve told Greg facts about the plane. He said the Spitfire was the RAF's most effective fighter plane in World War Two. German pilots were in awe of it and wanted to fly it themselves. Steve used the model to show Greg the main parts of the plane. The fuel tank behind the pilot's seat. The guns and ammo in the wings.

Steve was so passionate about it all that he made the little plastic plane interesting, even for Greg. Some of the time. But Greg couldn't help gazing into the woods out past the window. They still seemed to thrum with

those strange noises. And the room they were in felt strange too. An old clock chimed every 15 minutes. Everything was made of wood. It seemed very old fashioned, as if nothing had changed much since the days of the wartime pilots.

All too soon they had finished the plane, Steve stopped his chat and Greg was bored again. He had been thinking – while Steve fixed the wheels onto the Spitfire – that he could go to bed early and play on his phone. He could even go to sleep and set his alarm to wake him up so he could play in the night.

The clock struck eight and Greg stretched and yawned. "I think I'll go to bed."

"It's early," Esther said, with a question in her voice. "I thought we might play cards or something."

Maddie and Jess both stood up and said yes. Jatinder nodded too.

But Greg shook his head. "I'm tired," he said. "Maybe tomorrow?"

"OK," Esther said. "If you need anything, just call us. Even in the middle of the night."

Greg nodded, desperate to get out the room.

"Take the plane with you," Steve said. "And the paints. If you wake up early you could paint it. Just put some paper down first and follow the guide."

"Thanks," Greg said, but he knew he wouldn't. He was going to play on his phone. Any game but FightClub. But still he took the tray with the grey Spitfire, paints and brushes upstairs with him.

FIVE

It was 3 a.m. when Greg's alarm went off.

Game time. He picked up his phone.

"Eh?" Greg said, rubbing his eyes. The screen was blank.

'But it's plugged in,' he thought.

And it was. The phone was connected to the power, but it wasn't charging.

For 15 minutes, Greg tried to start it. He plugged it in and took it out, pressed two buttons at once, shook it. All the time, he was getting more and more frustrated.

At last he gave up. The phone was broken. He turned the light off and tried to go back to sleep. But that wouldn't work either. He was wide awake now, twitchy and restless. And he could hear those engine noises again, and see the flashing of lights outside.

In the end, Greg went over to the window, opened the curtains and looked out into the foggy dark. The moonlight was casting weird shadows around the house. He wondered if the RAF was doing some secret mission in the middle of the night. Did that even happen still?

Then he remembered the Spitfire model.

He'd paint it. Why not? What else was there to do?

Greg turned on the lights, sat down and looked at the guide that showed how to paint the plane. First the camouflage on the wings. He opened the green and brown paints, and as he painted, he was aware of the noises and lights still going on outside. He kept trying to work out what it was. It wasn't the RAF, secret mission or otherwise.

A carpark near by?

A motorway?

Whatever. Greg stopped worrying about it and focused on painting the plane. He did a coat of camouflage, then painted the tyres on the wheels and the propeller black. Then he stopped.

The plane looked OK, but not great. It was a bit smudgy, even though he'd tried hard to get it right. But he liked it. Its shape looked familiar. The rounded wings. The black propeller. He'd seen the plane on films and adverts. Even on one of his friend's T-shirts.

Greg turned to the window again.

What he saw astonished him. Light was streaming in the window and dazzling him. There was a deafening noise of engines revving. And that smell of fuel or oil that he'd smelled while out on the airfield with Steve.

Then Greg heard a rattling sound like a display of fireworks going off all at once. He clasped his hands to his ears as a chill wind swept around his room. He jumped to one side – it was as if someone was driving an invisible machine through the house.

What was going on?

Greg pushed the curtains fully open, then stumbled backwards in amazement.

Shafts of light stood like pillars in the mist, with shapes moving to and fro between them. And then – as he peered closer – Greg saw the plane he'd spotted in the woods the day before. The one he'd dismissed as the shadows of branches. He could see now that it was no such thing. It was a Spitfire. A full-sized Spitfire with a sharp-pointed nose and curved wings.

Greg steadied himself on the table next to the Airfix model as the shadowy shapes outside moved faster and faster, the lights glaring brighter and brighter and the noise of the engines growing ever louder.

SIX

Greg shielded his eyes from the light. The noise became too loud to bear, and he grabbed a pair of headphones and slipped them over his ears.

Headphones?

He opened his eyes and realised everything had changed.

Everything.

Greg was no longer at his window looking out at the airfield. No longer in his bedroom at Trenchard House at 3.30 a.m. He was in the cockpit of a plane. And that plane was a Spitfire.

He looked out of the canopy window, and saw that he was diving down fast towards the sea.

Plane?

Sea?

Diving?

It felt like he was falling. The way he was being pushed back in his seat. The way he couldn't focus on anything ahead of him or around him because the light and colours were rushing past him at such a speed.

Greg was frantic as he looked around the cockpit. What was happening? What could he do? He grabbed what looked like a control stick in front of him, moved it towards him, shifted it a fraction to the left.

As the plane responded, Greg stared at the layers of clouds in the sky and the huge expanse of sea. He was no longer diving. The plane was steady. Greg had no idea how he had done that, how he knew what to do. But he had. He had controlled the plane.

Then he heard a terrible sound.

"MUUUUUUUMMMMMMMM."

It took Greg a few seconds to work out that the terrible sound was him. It was him crying out for his mum.

And, even as he realised that, Greg knew that there was no point calling for his mum. This was really happening. It wasn't a dream. He wasn't going to wake up in bedsheets tangled with terror. He was in a Spitfire hurtling along above the sea.

'No,' he thought again, 'I can't be in a plane. I can't be piloting it.' Greg had played plenty of fighter pilot video games before, but this was no game.

Or was it?

Greg's mind scrabbled for meaning. He felt out of control, as if he might be very sick any second now. He was shaking. He opened and closed his eyes, each time hoping to change the reality around him. He could feel a freezing wind rushing in the gap in the glass pane in front of him. See flashes of green and white and black and blue zooming past and smell petrol. He could hear the roar of the engine and the wind bursting in at him. He had lost control of the plane again.

There was a scattering of black dots ahead, which he saw were the outlines of a dozen ships on the water far below.

"Control to blue section." The boom of a muffled voice came through the headphones on

Greg's flying helmet. "Bandits at 12 o'clock low. Three enemy bogies. Angels twelve. Attack."

Greg had no idea what the voice was saying, what these words meant, but somehow he knew that this was an assault. Other Spitfires were around his plane now, shifting in and out of the clouds as they grouped into formation to attack.

Within seconds Greg and the other Spitfires were heading into battle, and a swarm of Stukas were diving at the convoy of British ships.

Stukas? Where had that word come from? The name of the German planes was there in his mind, but he had no memory of ever being told about them.

Greg just watched, at first, as three of his fellow Spitfire pilots went in after the Stukas. But it was too late. The Stukas had released their bombs and were turning up out of their dives, heading back towards land in the distance that Greg realised must be France.

Greg watched the Stuka bombs fall, and he smiled as they missed the ships, hit the sea and exploded.

But then he saw another Stuka bomber start its dive. It was heading straight for a ship that was trailing behind the others.

Greg pushed his control stick forward to begin his own dive. Using all the speed that his Spitfire had, he wanted to cut the Stuka bomber off before it hit the ship.

He didn't think, didn't wonder how he knew what to do. He just did it. He had no time to think.

The Stuka was screaming closer and closer to the ship, about to release its bomb with sudden, fatal force. Greg aimed at a point just beyond the German plane. Then, as it passed

in front of him, ready to drop its bomb and sink the ship, Greg fired his machine guns and a deadly stream of bullets rattled out from his wings.

Greg fired and fired until he had used all his ammo and he saw the sea rushing fast towards him, forcing him out of his dive to gain some height.

At first all he could see was smoke. But, as the smoke cleared, he saw two things.

The ships steaming north, unharmed.

A black cloud of fire, which was the burning shell of the Stuka bomber as it sank into the sea.

He'd done it.

Done what? Shot down a German plane.

So – now what?

Greg looked over the edge of his plane. All he could see was sea. No land like he'd seen before. No Britain. No France. It was ridiculous, but he was lost.

"Which way do I go?" he said out loud.

He looked at his fuel gauge. He was surprised he even knew where it was. But somehow he did, just like he knew – as if by instinct – how to fly this plane.

The needle was pointing at the bottom of the dial. Greg was going to run out of fuel soon.

He scanned the horizon, looking along the edge of the sea for land.

And there, to his left, he saw a smudge on the line of the horizon. Land – perhaps?

He moved his control stick and felt his plane ease to the left. Now he was head on towards that smudge. He pushed the control stick forward and felt the plane sink to a level height above the sea.

This felt good. He could do it.

Like a game.

Maybe it was a game. Maybe he was in a game. Maybe he was in so deep that it felt real.

Then Greg heard a faint thrum over the sound of his own engine. He wasn't alone in the sky.

To his left and to his right were two more planes. They were green and brown, but they weren't the same shape as his plane. They had square wings and brutal black crosses under the pilot's cockpit and on the tail.

Germans Messerschmitts.

Greg was a sitting target. He was out of fuel and ammo, and they had him exactly where they wanted him.

Greg looked around his cockpit, desperate to find a way to defend himself. He touched his leg and noticed a pistol in a holster at his side.

Could he use that? From his cockpit? No. Probably not.

Greg was at the mercy of the German planes.

SEVEN

Greg looked to his left and then to his right. The two German planes were flanking him. It could only mean one thing.

Death.

He imagined the planes turning towards him and firing a hail of bullets at his Spitfire. And then everything would be over. That's what he had done to the Stuka pilot. This was war. And, in war, these German pilots would do the same to him.

But, instead, one of them waved to him, pointed down to the land below and then went ahead of Greg's Spitfire. The other German plane moved in behind him.

In a flash, Greg worked out what was going on.

'They're bringing me in,' he thought. 'They're taking me prisoner.'

Greg did what he knew the German pilots wanted. Better to be a prisoner than to fall to earth in a twisted metal ball of fire.

He eased his plane lower, towards the green spread of fields below. After a few minutes he saw what he knew was an airfield. As the plane descended, Greg's mind was all over the place. Why the Germans would do that?

'To save my life,' was one thought he had.

But that seemed unlikely. They had been shooting down planes all day. Why save him?

'To torture me?' was a second thought.

Maybe that was it. Maybe they wanted to get information out of him. And then it came to him, just as he made his perfect landing – wheels down, control stick back.

His plane. The Spitfire.

That was why they were bringing him in. The Spitfire had ruled the skies in World War Two. "Dominated" – that was the word Steve had used. He'd talked about the Spitfire's powerful engine, its rounded wings – and how fast and agile it was. How its incredible firepower made it a perfect killing machine.

Greg realised how much the Germans could learn if they captured his plane rather than shot it down from the sky.

"No way," he said out loud. "No way will my Spitfire fall into enemy hands."

The engine of the Spitfire growled to a halt and Greg pulled back the canopy. As he climbed onto the wing, he took the gun from the holster at his side.

He knew this was dangerous. All around him were muddy, churned up roads and fields filled with German planes, air crews and vehicles. Everyone was looking at him, and as soon as he took his gun out he saw them turn their rifles and pistols on him. Any of them could shoot him just like that.

But Greg was steely sure. His mind was fixed. It was his plane and the enemy wasn't going to have it. No way.

This was it. This was his moment. Do or die.

Greg jumped off the plane, rolled onto the ground and fired a bullet into the Spitfire's petrol tank. Then he scrambled to his feet and ran.

The blast flung him hard across the muddy grass.

The boom made him deaf.

He lay pinned to the ground, and his head spun.

What had he done? He had destroyed his plane – it was blown to pieces – but what had he done to himself? Was he about to be punished, executed, tortured? He had no idea.

Greg's thoughts span away from him into darkness as he passed out.

The next thing Greg felt was a hand on his arm. He kept his eyes closed, unsure what was coming next.

His head still felt full of a whirling, dizzy fog. His arm stung with a sharp pain.

Then a harsh voice spoke.

"Open your eyes. You will not come to harm." The accent was German. "You are a prisoner of war," the voice went on. "Please, your name?"

"Greg ..." Greg found it hard to speak. His throat was dry and his ears were ringing. "Tomasze– ... Gregory Thomas." Greg's name was Grzegorz Tomaszewski, but instinct told him to make his name sound English for these men.

The German soldier narrowed his eyes at Greg, then looked down at Greg's arm. "You have an injury from your fall, Officer Thomas. Please, let us see to it. We have a medical kit in the truck. We will make you more comfortable. Yes?"

"Yes," Greg replied. "Thank you."

"Come."

Greg wanted to ask where exactly they were going, but pain was pulsing through him in waves, making him want to do or say as little as possible. He closed his eyes – bearing it – and hoped that this German soldier meant what he said.

EIGHT

Cold morning light had begun to seep through
the window of the truck transporting Greg. He
was desperate for sleep, but his arm was agony,
and every jolt and bump in the road made him
want to vomit.

Then the truck stopped with a judder.

Next Greg heard sharp voices outside. As
he waited, anxious, he stared at a piece of cloth
he'd found in one of his pockets. At first he'd
thought it was an old-fashioned hankie, but
now he could see it was a map printed on a
piece of silk. It was a map of Europe, but the
borders and the names of some of the countries

were different from the ones he'd learned at school.

The vehicle began to inch forward again.

'We're driving through a gate,' Greg thought. 'We've arrived.'

Greg's body flooded with fear and he felt himself start to sweat and shake. He could feel how very different his body was now. Here, in this place, he was an adult, a man with heavy muscles on his arms and legs, a face rough with stubble, deeper sounds in his throat when he coughed and spoke. But he was still Greg. Inside.

Then a soldier with a gun slung over his back opened the door. There was another soldier behind him, his gun pointing at Greg.

"*Raus!*" the soldier barked, and he shoved Greg to make him move.

It took Greg's eyes a while to adjust to the light outside. He was in a clearing in a forest, thousands of tall trees spread over a hillside that seemed to stretch for miles. In the clearing, dozens of wooden huts stood in rows, all surrounded by a tall barbed wire fence. The sun was coming up, casting shadows across the grid of huts and the narrow paths between them.

"*Raus!*"

Greg followed his armed guard to a hut, where a man was sitting. The man was tall with broad shoulders, and he had a prowling look in his eyes like that of a caged tiger. He wore three bands on his shoulder and he half-smiled as he stood to greet Greg.

"Welcome to Stalag Luft VC," he said, in a Scottish accent. "This is a prison camp."

Without thinking about it, Greg felt himself raise his hand to salute the other man.

The man saluted back. "I'm Squadron Leader Strachan, senior British officer here," he said. "Just landed?"

"Yes, sir," Greg replied. "I ... er ... I need to explain."

"Your name, officer?"

"Erm." Greg's voice caught in his throat. "Greg. Greg Thomas."

"Gregor? Gregory?"

Greg took a deep breath to steady his voice. He had to get this right. Nobody could know he had a Polish name. The German soldiers would treat him very differently if they knew. "Everyone calls me Greg," he managed to say.

The Squadron Leader ignored Greg's answer and instead looked at his arm.

"We need to get that arm sorted," he said. "I assume you injured it coming down?"

"Yes, sir," Greg said. He could feel a horrible wave of panic breaking over him. Would he ever get anyone to understand?

"Spitfire?" Strachan said.

"Sorry, sir?"

"Did you come down in a Spitfire?" Strachan asked. "Or a Lancaster?"

"A Spitfire, I think, sir."

"You think?" Squadron Leader Strachan laughed. "Don't you know what you were flying?"

Now was the time for Greg to explain. He had to.

"The thing is, sir, I'm not a pilot. I'm a boy. I'm twelve years old. I was making a model of a Spitfire, and next thing I was in a plane that was crashing into the sea. And … and now I'm here and I just want to get home."

Greg felt Strachan's hand on his back. "Sit down, airman," Strachan said. "You're in shock. The crash. And your arm. It may be infected. Poison in the blood can play tricks with your mind."

"No," Greg insisted, as the pain in his arm swelled to a relentless throb. "I'm just a boy. It's all a mistake …"

Greg was aware that a couple more men were now standing near them. One wore a thick jumper and one was in a flying jacket. They were talking to each other in low voices.

"He's gone daft, Tom," Strachan said to one of them. "Shock of the crash. Talking all sorts of drivel."

"But the Germans escorted him down," the other man said. "He didn't crash. They wanted to capture his Spitfire. But he blew it up to stop them. Shot at the tank. Close range."

"Impossible," Strachan said. "He'd be killed."

"Impossible, yes, but he's alive."

Strachan laughed. "My God. Give the man a medal. What a way to keep the Spitfire out of enemy hands."

"Forget medals," the third man said. "His arm needs seeing to. Get the Doc, will you?"

Greg could only listen now as the other men's voices faded in and out. He was too tired. He gave up on trying to explain himself and allowed them to take him to a wooden hut at the far end of the prison camp.

NINE

Greg opened his eyes and stared at the man in the thick jumper who had helped him the night before, and then at the room around him. Wooden slats for walls, a stove in the corner, bunk beds with blankets that looked like old sacks. That was about it.

"Ahh, you're awake, Thomas," the man said as Greg closed his eyes again. "Good. How does the arm feel? Would you like a cup of tea?"

'A cup of tea?' Greg thought. 'What good will that do?'

His eyes felt hot and his throat tight. He was trying so hard not to cry that it was hard to breathe. What would they think of him if he cried? He was supposed to be a man. And not just an ordinary man, but a fighter pilot in the RAF.

He kept his eyes closed, and heard a scraping noise on the floor. Then he felt someone sitting next to him.

"I'm Nokes," the man said. "Tom Nokes."

Greg opened his eyes and studied Nokes. He was a big man with light hair and kind blue eyes. His Yorkshire accent was comforting.

"Greg," Greg said. "Greg Thomas." He looked at the man's bulky bandaged hands.

"You noticed my hands? I ... I er ... cut them," Nokes explained. "You know."

Greg nodded and eased himself into a sitting position on the edge of the bottom bunk.

"I hear you came down in a Spit – blew it up," Nokes said. "Two days ago? You've been asleep for 36 hours since you got here."

"Have I?" Greg asked.

"You must feel pretty cut up, blowing it up like that," Nokes said. "Even Fritz is impressed."

"Cut up is about right," Greg said, and he wanted to cry again.

"I parachuted out of a Lancaster," Nokes told him. "Came down in a farm yard. A soft landing in the you-know-what. Never been so glad of a pile of manure in my life."

Greg laughed. He forgot about crying and felt very glad of this man's friendly, funny company.

"How's the patient, Nokes?" A man Greg had not seen before had arrived in the hut.

"He's doing well, aren't you, Thomas?" Nokes said.

Greg nodded.

"This is Batty," Nokes told Greg. "He's the Doc. Sorted your arm after you passed out. How is it looking, Batty?"

"Fine," Batty said. "Your arm will hurt for a while, Thomas, but apart from that you'll be right as rain. In a few days you'll be climbing over the fences and running into the woods. You'll be our number one escapee."

The three men fell silent as Greg thought about what Batty had said. Could he escape? Could he find his way home? The idea was the first thing to lift his spirits since this whole nightmare had begun.

Batty crouched next to Greg, and the tone of his voice was different, less bluff now. "How do you feel, Thomas ... you know ... inside?"

Greg looked at Batty's round face and smart moustache. He looked like a photo of a man from the olden days. But Greg knew what he was asking. He wanted to know if Greg still thought he was a boy from more than 70 years after the war. Or, to put it another way, was he still mad?

"The same," Greg said, his voice firm. "I feel the same inside."

"I see," the doctor said. "Well, it might take a while for you to feel better."

"There's no better about it," Greg snapped. "I am Greg Thomas. I'm twelve years old. From the 21st century."

Greg saw Nokes and Batty exchange a glance. The kind of glance that said, 'This man is crazy. Let's keep an eye on him.'

Then Greg had an idea, a way that he could prove he was from the future.

"We win, you know," he said, and he looked Nokes and Batty in the eye.

"Win what, old man?" Batty asked.

"The war," Greg said. "We win the war."

"Do we? Good show."

Greg shook his head. They were still treating him like a fool. He pressed on, scrabbling together what he remembered from History lessons. "The Germans try to invade Britain in 1940, but they fail," he told them. "Then the Americans join in, on our side. And the war ends in 1945 when the Russian Army take Poland and capture Berlin. Hitler dies in a bunker and Germany surrenders."

"That's some story," Tom Nokes said, with a frown at Batty. "Five years more. Oh dear. I was rather hoping to be home for the summer."

'It's no joke!' Greg thought. How could he get them to take him seriously?

Science. That was it. He'd tell them about sci-fi stuff that would happen in their future.

"Americans walk on the moon in 1969," he said.

"I see." Batty nodded. "How will they manage that?"

'It's no joke!' Greg thought. How could he get them to take him seriously?

Greg tried again. "There's a space station that circles the Earth – I think Russians live on it –"

"What? All of them?" Nokes said. "That space station must be pretty big ..."

"No," Greg almost shouted, angry now. "Just two or three astronauts."

Batty was no longer smiling. He was looking at Greg with worry on his face.

Greg stopped. "You think I'm mad, don't you?" he asked.

Batty spoke with compassion. "You've blown a plane up. You've had your arm half ripped off. You're in a fever. You just need rest."

"I'm a twelve-year-old boy," Greg muttered, "not an airman."

Batty turned to Nokes. "Pass me that mirror, will you?"

Nokes did as he was asked and Batty held the mirror up to Greg.

Greg looked and saw a man with dark rings around his eyes and deep scratches on his face. He put his hand up to touch his face. A man's hand appeared in the mirror. It was clear why nobody believed he was a boy.

TEN

It was Greg's tenth day in Stalag Luft VC.

His arm was a lot better and boredom
was the big pain for him now. Day after day
of nothing to do, just sitting outside the huts,
waiting for nothing to happen. Gazing at the
huts and the woods, and at the fences between
the two. Watching the German guards walking
the perimeter of the prison camp. Longing
for the space and freedom that lay beyond the
barbed wire fences.

Greg had become used to the fact that he
was an RAF airman, that it was 1940 and World
War Two had not long started. Also that he was
a prisoner and might never go home again. It

was weird, being a man rather than a child. Greg had to shave the rough hair off his face every day and wash as often as he could to stop the sour smell of sweat that built up in the heat.

Everyone else in the camp had been plucked from their lives and families too and – like Greg – they were stuck here with nothing to do. Today Nokes and Batty were sitting in the shade outside their hut, talking, just like the day before and the day before that. But when Greg joined them, they stopped talking and Nokes rubbed out a diagram he had sketched in the dusty floor with his boot. Greg could feel Batty studying him, looking to see if he had noticed.

Greg knew what the diagram was – and why the other two wanted to hide it from him. It was an escape plan. He had worked that much out. But he said nothing. Greg knew that nobody talked about escape – not unless they wanted to be involved. There was no other way to keep plans secret.

The three men sat and watched two deer on the edge of the woods beyond the fence, their coats red in the sunshine. But as a guard walked along the perimeter, his footsteps startled the deer and they skittered off into the safety of the trees.

Greg found that he felt as jumpy as those deer. He wasn't sure what it was, but tension was building in the camp. The other prisoners were not acting quite as normal. In fact, they were acting a little too normal. They were watching, but pretending not to watch, and looking busy while doing nothing.

There was something going on in the camp.

Greg saw some soldiers loading a truck with rubbish and old mattresses. That was what everyone was watching while they pretended not to. Greg wondered what everyone was holding their breath for.

Maybe a guard would fall off the truck?

Maybe the truck's engine would overheat in the sun?

They all wanted something out of the ordinary to happen. It didn't matter what. Anything to break the seal of tension building around them.

Greg sat forward, and his heart beat faster.

When at last the truck was loaded, it began to move off. But as soon as it did so, the German camp commandant appeared from nowhere and walked into its path. The silver buttons and rows of medals on his jacket glinted as he held up his hand.

"HALT!" he commanded.

Everyone watched in silence as he ordered one of his soldiers up onto the truck and ordered him to stab each mattress with his bayonet.

Greg swallowed. Was a prisoner hidden in one of the mattresses? The long sharp blade on the end of the soldier's gun could skewer a man. He wanted to shout out and save whoever was hiding in the mattresses, if there was someone. But he knew that if he did shout, he would give the escapee away. So, like everyone else, he sat there and watched in horror as he waited for the bayonet to stab the hidden man.

It didn't take long.

There was a sudden shout of "Hier ist er!"

Five or six German soldiers swarmed onto the back of truck.

Nokes and Batty stood to see more, and Greg jumped up too.

And there he was. A man as white as a sheet with his hands in the air, and a stream of blood pouring from his arm.

No one reacted as he was led away. The other prisoners were still and silent with horror. They all knew where he was going – solitary confinement. A cell where he would be kept alone for days. A cell with little to eat, little to drink and only cockroaches and mice for company. Solitary was his punishment, and a warning to the rest of the men.

"Nokes?" Greg whispered.

"Yes, old man?"

"I want to help you," Greg said. "Whatever you're doing I want to be part of it."

"Good show," Batty said. "You look strong enough. Are you handy with a shovel? There's a tunnel to be dug."

ELEVEN

Batty was right. Greg was stronger than he could ever have imagined. And so he was given the role of digger.

Digging the tunnel was harder than anything Greg had ever known, but his muscles seemed to have almost unlimited energy and power. But there was more to it than that. He enjoyed getting stuck into something after the days of boredom, feeling determined to finish.

Every day the digging was the same. The men would pull away the stove at the back of their hut and crawl down the hole underneath into the dark, with a small candle lantern to light their way. They'd go down a rickety ladder made of wooden slats from their bunk beds. Then Greg would have to get on his hands and knees to crawl along the dirty, airless tunnel.

Greg hadn't been a prisoner as long as the others, so he was still lean and strong rather than skinny from camp rations. He dug with a large tin can that had been cut across the top and welded to form a small hand-shovel. It wasn't great, but it had to do. From the first day his hands blistered and his nails cracked, but Nokes showed him how to look after them so they didn't get infected like his own had. It was Nokes's job to take up the soil and rock that Greg dug away, then scatter it under Batty's medical hut when it was safe to do so.

Sometimes Greg lay and dug on his back, and sometimes on his front. He had to change every now and then to avoid the pain and cramps caused by working in one position for too long. Every day he excavated one yard of tunnel in a six-hour shift. All he had was a small cup of water to keep his throat from drying up from all the dusty soil around him.

Hour after hour. Day after day. They knew it would take time, and inch by inch they progressed.

*

Four weeks into the digging, Greg was sitting at the side of the hut, waiting to do another shift in the tunnel. His arms still hurt from the night before.

"Two or three more nights," Nokes muttered under his breath. "Then we'll be out in those woods. We'll be running away from this hell-hole of a camp like those deer."

Greg nodded, and the memory of the deer drew his eyes to the barbed wire fence. A prisoner was kneeling down there, tying his shoe laces.

He was looking around at the guards, wanting to see their reaction.

Greg and Nokes stopped speaking and watched.

An escape was on. You could just tell.

All of a sudden another prisoner shot out like a racehorse from between two of the men's huts. His arms and legs were moving like pistons and he picked up speed so fast that by the time he reached the kneeling man, he was almost flying.

Then the kneeling man lifted his shoulders as the sprinting man reached him. The sprinter jumped onto his back and hurled himself over the fence. He had used the kneeling man as a springboard, to give him the lift he needed to vault over the fence. It was a spectacular piece of gymnastics.

Then the sprinter was in a heap on the other side of the fence. He lay there for a second, then, as a German soldier shouted "Halt! Halt!", he was up on his feet again, running towards the first trees.

Now the whole prison camp was standing, shouting and cheering, swarming towards the fence, desperate to see this man make it to the woods. To find his freedom and to taste that freedom for them all. He was half way to the trees when the first sentry fired his gun.

"Run!" the prisoners shouted from behind the fence. "Go on, mate!"

Greg stood there, grinning fit to burst, caught up in the buzz of an escape, caught up in everyone's hope that they weren't trapped in this endless boredom for ever.

The man was even closer to the woods now. As he got further away from the sentries' rifles, he became ever harder to shoot at. He ran in zig zags, making a precise aim impossible.

'Freedom,' Greg thought. 'He's so close to freedom.'

"RUN!" he shouted one last time as the rattle of machine guns exploded from one of the sentry towers above the camp. Greg saw the man speed up for three or four steps, stumble, then hit the ground in a slump.

"No!" Greg shouted, and his heart almost banged its way out of his chest. "No! Get up!"

But the man didn't get up.

"Get up," Greg said, but lower this time. He knew there was no chance.

Greg sat down and gazed at the ground. He scraped his foot across the dry soil, then scraped it back again. Inside he was raging. He wanted to attack the guards that had killed the prisoner. But that was pointless. He could only sit there seething.

The mood in the camp turned desperate. Men couldn't look each other in the eye. They were grieving for the dead airman and for all their hopes of freedom.

Nokes sat down next to Greg. "Let's give the tunnel a miss tonight," he muttered.

"No," Greg said. "We dig. Every night we dig until we're out of this hell."

Nokes turned to him with a smile.

"What?" Greg asked. "There's nothing to smile about."

"You're right, there isn't," Nokes said. "But what I like about you is that you never give up."

TWELVE

They were ready.

It was the evening of the escape attempt.

Batty had measured the tunnel as best he could to make sure it would reach the trees. They had come up against a tangle of tree roots, so they couldn't dig any further anyway.

Under their uniforms, all three men were wearing the closest thing they could get to working men's clothes. They had on their airmen's boots. When they were on the outside, those could be cut down to look like normal boots.

It was a windy night, with plenty of cloud. Perfect. The wind would cover up any noise they made as they scrambled out of the tunnel. The cloud would hide the light of the moon, and that would make them less visible to the German soldiers.

They collected their last meal of the day and sat together on the steps of their hut with the mugs of soup and chunks of heavy brown bread.

Greg was so nervous he had hadn't touched his food.

"Eat it," Nokes said.

"I can't swallow," Greg told him.

"Eat it or the guards will suspect you."

Nokes was right – the guards were forever watching the men, looking for signs that something out of the ordinary was going on.

Greg frowned and bit into the dark bread. It was so dry he might as well have been eating soil from inside the tunnel.

*

Four hours later night had fallen, and Greg and Batty and Nokes were gathered at the hut.

Now all they had to do was wait for the guard to complete his rounds of the prison wire.

Greg looked at his friends and smiled. He trusted these men. He trusted their honest, brave faces, now coloured dark with mud. Their joint efforts to dig this tunnel had given him a purpose these last few weeks. Now all they needed was a little luck and they might be free.

Greg held his breath as the guard walked around the camp, afraid he would hear even that. But the guard passed by, noticing nothing.

They had drawn straws to decide who would be first out of the tunnel. No one was sure if being first was a good thing or not. First into the woods, if all went well. Or the first to be shot if it didn't.

Greg drew the shortest straw. He would be first.

One by one they scrambled under the stove and down into the tunnel. Soon they were crawling along on their hands and knees, lit by a lamp that Greg had fixed around his neck. It was breathless work, in air that was weak and dusty. This time, Greg didn't worry about keeping the dirt off his hands and face. The filthier his skin, the less chance the soldiers would spot him when they were out of the tunnel and in the woods.

But as the tunnel's tight walls pressed in on him, Greg felt a pounding sense of panic. His heart beat fast in fear that the tunnel might collapse, but he forced the thought away. He had to focus.

After nearly 100 yards of crawling, the tunnel rose bit by bit until it was nearly at the surface.

Tree roots scratched against Greg's knees as he hacked away at the last few inches of earth. He was about to break through the soil, about to escape. He'd imagined this moment for weeks, and he'd thought then he'd be so nervous that his hands would tremble. But, in fact, he was as calm as he'd ever been.

Greg worked slowly, not wanting to make unnecessary noise. If the guards heard a sound from the woods, they would soon discover the escapees. Greg gave silent thanks that it was a windy night. The brushing and clicking sounds in the branches and in the wire of the fence would help.

Greg worked until he saw tiny pinpricks of light above him. Stars. They looked brighter from outside the prison wire.

He snuffed out the lamp that had lit their way. Then he brushed away the remaining soil and made a hole big enough for the three of them to climb out one by one.

Greg turned to his friends and stuck his thumb up. He took in a deep breath.

This was it. The escape.

He knew the last thing he should do was hesitate, so he put both hands onto the edge of the hole and lifted himself out into the open air.

THIRTEEN

Greg's hands touched the dry soil and the tree roots of the forest floor. He was out of the tunnel. Next, he helped Nokes to climb out. Then, for a second, the two men stared back at the prison camp, checking it was safe for Batty.

The camp looked different from the outside. Smaller somehow. Greg could see two of the towers where German sentries stood with searchlights and machine guns, ready to fire at the slightest thing. But he felt safe in the dark. Unseen.

Greg was about to help Batty out of the hole when he heard it.

The ear-splitting wail of the camp siren.

Then a searchlight swept across the ground outside the wire fence. It was like some wild creature racing towards Greg and Nokes through the trees. Greg flinched as the light flashed over him and Nokes. Then it stopped and moved back the way it had come to catch them in its beam.

They'd been seen.

"Run," Batty shouted, as he ducked back into the hole. "Leave me."

There was nothing Greg and Nokes could do but run.

Greg sprinted as hard as he could. As he ran, he thought of the man who had vaulted over the fence and how he'd gone down with a line of bullets in his back. The thought made him run harder. His feet thumped on the forest

floor, bullets cracked off the trees, and all the time he expected a hot stab of pain in his back.

Greg felt like his lungs might collapse. He had never run like this before. Soon, it became too much and he stopped, ducking behind a tree for cover. He put his hands on his knees and tried to draw air into his lungs. He looked back and saw lights prowling the woods like animals, and flashes of bullets from guns.

Then Nokes was next to him.

"Keep going," Nokes gasped. "They're after us. The further we can get away, the better. These woods go on for ever. They'll never find us in here."

Greg knew Nokes was right. So he followed, trying to keep up, determined not to let Nokes down, not to give up. But the woods were dark and almost as soon as they began running again, Nokes stumbled over a tree root and Greg fell on top of him. And even though men with guns were plunging into the woods after them, they both laughed like children.

"Come on," Greg said. He pulled Nokes up, almost hugging him as they laughed.

Shouts.

Gunshots.

Trees lit up ahead of them.

"Torches," Nokes warned. "Run."

Greg and Nokes ran on, zig-zagging through the thick woods, desperate not be spotted.

Soon the land began to go downhill and Greg could hear a rushing noise, as if the wind was blowing harder. He slowed down as Nokes reduced his pace too.

"I have to rest," Nokes said, "just for two minutes."

Greg was glad Nokes wanted to stop. His own lungs were in agony and he could feel his leg muscles burning for lack of oxygen.

"Have we shaken them off?" Greg asked after a few moments. He was lying on the soft ground below the trees, filling his raw lungs with air.

"I hope so," Nokes whispered.

The vast woods settled quiet and still around them. There was just the rushing sound that Greg realised was a river or a stream, not the wind.

"What's happened to Batty?" Greg asked.

Nokes shook his head. "I'm not sure he came out. And, if he did ..."

"What?"

"He would have been a sitting duck."

Greg nodded. It was true. The two of them had gone alone into the woods.

But Greg couldn't think any more about Batty. There was nothing they could do for him now. And so he just focused on breathing, getting ready for the next stage of their escape.

But as Greg and Nokes lay there listening to the soft calls of the night birds and the rushing of the stream, they heard a new sound. It was far worse than the shouts of soldiers or the firing of guns.

"Dogs!" Nokes said, and cursed.

"Come on," Greg said. "We need to go. Now."

Dogs would pick up their scent from miles away.

FOURTEEN

Greg wasn't sure his body could take any more as he and Nokes ran on again. He was gasping for breath and the pain in his lungs was unbearable.

The idea came into his head that he could just stop running. He could lie down in these dark, damp woods, not even try to hide or shelter.

It would be so easy just to stop.

It would feel so good to give up and put an end to the pain.

Then a memory came to him. Of being bored at Steve and Esther's.

Of Hafeez being so disappointed that Greg had given up wanting to be a keeper.

And Greg knew that – whatever happened to him in the future – he would never give up again.

"The dogs are getting closer," Nokes warned, snapping Greg back to the present. "I can hear them. They'll catch us soon."

"The stream," Greg gasped. "If we run in the water the dogs will lose our scent."

Greg knew the stream would be downhill from where they stood. And there it was – at the foot of a slope.

The pair splashed down the centre of the stream, trying not to fall or twist their ankles on the stony river bed. At first, they could hear the dogs barking and growling, but, after a while, there was less noise from the dogs, and more shouts and curses from the guards chasing them. Then they could only hear their own footsteps splashing in the shallow water.

"Over there," Nokes said, grabbing Greg to stop him, and pointing east.

Greg looked.

For the first time he could see the trees properly as they formed black silhouettes against the sky. Pale light glowed behind them.

"The sun's coming up," Nokes said. "We need to hide. We need to travel by night, sleep by day."

And so, Greg and Nokes slept during the day and walked at night. They worked their slow way south to the Swiss border, through forests and over mountains, using the silk map Greg had found in his pocket after he'd landed his Spitfire as a guide. He was glad he'd kept it. Switzerland was a neutral country, on neither side in the war. That meant, if they could get across its border, they would be free to fly home.

As the two men walked, they talked about their lives back home. Nokes had been a trainee policeman before the war and wanted to go back on the beat in North Yorkshire. When Nokes asked about Greg's life, Greg told him the same thing he always had – that he had been a boy in the 21st century. He told Nokes detail after detail – about history, technology, books and football and everyday life. Nokes listened without arguing. But Greg knew that he never really believed him. Of course he didn't. How could he?

After four days, Greg and Nokes reached the German–Swiss border. It had been raining for hours and they were soaked to the skin. Their filthy clothes hung heavy on their weary bodies and their rough boots had rubbed the raw skin off their feet.

What they saw did nothing to cheer them. This border was a deep, fast-flowing river. There were German guards and military vehicles posted for miles in either direction. The only way across was the road bridge that looked to be as heavily guarded as the prison camp they had escaped from.

Getting out of Germany was not going to be a stroll through a field of buttercups and into the sunshine. In fact, it would be much harder than their escape from the prison camp.

"Now what?" Greg said. "How on earth do we tackle that?"

"We'll find a way," Nokes replied. "I promise you. One day we'll kneel down and kiss the earth at home."

FIFTEEN

It was dark when Greg and Nokes made their move.

They'd found a good hiding place – a dense clump of bushes, just 50 yards from the wooden bridge over the river. There, they sheltered from the rain until night fell.

The rain of the last few days meant that the water in the wild, fast river that separated Germany and Switzerland was as high and dangerous as it could be. They would be washed away if they tried to swim across.

And so Greg watched the bridge carefully. It was guarded by ranks of German troops, but it was their only option. As the sun set, Greg noticed trucks passing now and then between the two countries. Each truck had to stop on this side of the barrier to have their passports and papers checked before they moved on into Switzerland.

That was the answer.

"What if ..." Greg stopped and watched how the German soldiers checked the inside of the truck, but nothing else.

"What if what?" Nokes asked.

Greg told Nokes his plan. A plan that, if it worked, would take them to the Swiss side of the border in a few minutes. If it failed, they would be dead.

When the next truck approached the bridge, Greg and Nokes crawled from their hideout to the edge of the road. Once the truck had stopped at the barrier, the two men rolled

underneath it, grabbing at the undercarriage for parts to cling onto.

Greg didn't let himself listen to the thump of his heart rate picking up in panic.

It was a risk. A crazy thing to do. But it was the only way.

Greg found places to jam his feet and a pipe to hold onto. But, as the truck's engine revved, ready to move on, he saw that Nokes was still struggling to find a hand-hold. Everything was red-hot from the heat of the engine.

"I can't ..." Nokes gasped, as the truck began to move off. He was there on the road, helpless, with a pair of thick tyres rolling straight at him.

Greg saw the desperate, terrified look in Nokes's eyes. He held out his leg and shouted above the noise of the engine. "Grab it!"

Nokes snatched at Greg's leg. Now Greg was bearing all Nokes's weight as he was dragged along by the truck.

The pain in Greg's arms and legs was incredible. The arm that he'd injured a few weeks ago felt like it was on fire, as if it was being pushed further and further into a furnace. It was a mercy that the truck was moving so slowly, but the pain was so fierce that Greg had to fight with himself not to let go of the truck. He knew that if he didn't hold on for dear life, he and Nokes would be dropped into the middle of the road, still in Germany, with dozens of soldiers ready to take them both prisoner again. Or kill them there and then.

With each second that passed, Greg felt Nokes's arms slip further down his leg.

"Hold on," Greg shouted. "Please hold on." And, somehow, urging Nokes to be strong gave Greg strength too.

He held on. Nokes held on.

'Just a few more seconds now,' Greg told himself. 'Hold on, for God's sake. Hold on.'

He closed his eyes.

And when he opened them again and looked down, the road was not road any more. It was wood. His hands slipped. He felt Nokes's arms slipping away from his feet. He felt himself hit the bridge.

Greg braced himself. Were they still in Germany? Or in a no-man's-land? Or safe in Switzerland? Would they be shot or would they walk away as free men?

When he dared to look round, Greg saw several pairs of heavy army boots standing around him. His head was still on the ground. He was surrounded by troops.

Greg stood before Nokes did. Two soldiers were coming towards him, both holding rifles.

He heard the click of a gun's safety catch.

Then one of the soldiers spoke. "Welcome to Switzerland."

Greg dropped back onto his knees and laughed out loud. His laughter turned to sobs as he put his arms round Nokes.

SIXTEEN

Greg and Nokes were on their way home to England. It was three days after they had fallen from under the truck and into Switzerland.

Greg sat opposite his friend and smiled, but neither of them spoke. They were nearly free. Nearly home. But neither of them was going to celebrate – neither of them would believe it was true – until they were safely back in Britain.

Greg gazed out of the window at the sea below. As he stared, he dreamed of home.

When at last the plane made it over the sea and dropped down towards the English coast, Greg felt a burst of joy. He wanted to laugh and shout and sing. But he waited – for that moment when he would kiss the surface of the airfield. He and Nokes had spoken about that moment so often.

But, as they were landing, Greg wanted to cry with frustration. Everything was not going to be OK. The airfield was just a grass runway and wooden huts. It was, of course, 1940. They were landing in an England at war. An England of over 75 years ago.

Greg was still trapped in the past. He was still as far from home and the football school as when he had been in the prison camp back in Germany.

It was home, but not in his time – and that thought was almost impossible to cope with.

But Greg was desperate not to spoil the moment for Nokes, so he tried not to cry, or shout or scream his fears. And when Nokes went down on his knees on the grass at the side of the runway and kissed the ground, Greg did the same. He was thinking of his new friend, wanting him to enjoy his homecoming at least.

He would deal with his own disappointment later.

As Greg at last raised his face from the grass, he felt the soft touch of a hand on his shoulder.

"Greg? Greg? Are you OK?"

Greg opened his eyes. Whose voice was that? Did he know it?

It wasn't Nokes's voice.

"Are you OK, son?" the voice said again.

"Sort of," Greg said, as he felt the hand pat his shoulder again. "I'm sort of OK." He hauled himself up and found himself looking into Steve's kind brown eyes. He was back. In Britain. In the 21st century.

"Where's Nokes?" he asked Steve.

"Nokes?" Steve said. "Who's Nokes?"

"My friend. We ..." Greg choked on a sob.

"Take it easy, mate," Steve said. "You must have had a bad dream – you were shouting in your sleep. But you're OK."

Greg nodded and looked out of his window. The woods were dark. No lights, no engines roaring. No stink of petrol filling the air.

He looked around the room, seeing it as if for the first time. He stared at the Spitfire model on the table.

"You did a good job," Steve said. He picked up the Spitfire and studied it.

"Maybe," Greg replied. "I must have."

He could hardly speak, he felt so confused. About where he was. About what had happened.

He stared again at Steve holding the Spitfire. His mind was starting to process it all. He was back at Steve and Esther's house. The Spitfire in Steve's hands was just a model. And Nokes was ... what? A dream? A ghost? Whatever he was, Greg wanted to know where he had gone and what had become of him.

"You've done a fine job," Steve said again. "The detail is perfect. It looks like the real thing."

"It is." Greg took the model from Steve. "It is the real thing." Greg gazed at it in amazement and his eyes filled with tears. It was a beautiful plane. Its shape. Its colours. What it had done.

"What is it, son?" Steve asked. His voice was full of concern.

"Something happened," Greg said and paused, uncertain of where to go next with his story. "It's hard to explain," he went on. "You wouldn't believe it."

"Try me," Steve said.

SEVENTEEN

Greg told Steve about the air battle above the sea with the Stukas, the way he was brought into land, the wooden huts and tall barbed wire of the prison camp, the escape tunnel and the trek across Germany with Nokes.

They sat up until morning together, and Steve listened to Greg's every word. Then he said Greg should sleep on it. He could think about it better once he was rested. Greg knew Steve hoped he'd think it had all been a dream. And he was right – how could it have been anything else?

Greg looked again at his model plane. It was exactly the same as last night. It was still painted green and brown, with perfect red, white and blue circles on the wings like targets. Roundels. That's what those circles were called. And Greg wondered – how did he know that?

He sat bolt upright.

How could this be? The plane looked just like a real plane. No way had Greg done that. His efforts at painting had been clumsy and messy. Did that mean the whole Spitfire adventure, the prison camp, his friendship with Nokes – and everything else – had really happened?

Greg fumbled for his phone. It worked now.

Greg found the RAF Museum website and searched. The one he'd been to with Steve and Jatinder.

His hands were shaking. His throat was tight, like he was about to cry. But he blocked those feelings out. There was something he had to know.

He found information about Spitfires and the RAF, about the German prison camps. He browsed black and white photos of pilots and planes and camps. He flicked past portrait after portrait – more focused even than when he was gaming – until he looked straight into a pair of intelligent blue eyes.

It was him.

Nokes.

His friend, Tom Nokes.

Greg gasped in disbelief as he read the writing about Nokes that was next to his portrait.

TOM NOKES
After walking across Germany to the Swiss border, Tom Nokes was flown with several

other escapees back to England. He was one of the first men to make a successful home run from Nazi Germany. During the rest of the war he trained Lancaster pilots and gunners.

After the war Nokes worked as a police officer in Harrogate, North Yorkshire.

Nokes was awarded the Distinguished Flying Cross medal for his bravery. In interviews, he said his medal was for not just for himself. He claimed that he escaped with another man. They had tunnelled out of Stalag Luft VC, walked across Germany and found their way into Switzerland together.

Nokes said that this other man had saved his life more than once and that without him he would never have made it home. He also said that this man had disappeared when they arrived back in England.

The other man's name, Nokes said, was Greg Thomas. He said he had tried to track him down but had never found a trace of him. His one regret in life was that he had never been reunited with Greg Thomas.

Tom Nokes died, aged 94, in Masham, North Yorkshire, leaving behind a wife and a son, Greg.

EIGHTEEN

Greg woke up starving, as if he really had spent a week walking across Germany living on berries and water from streams. He wolfed down slice after slice of hot toast at breakfast, while Steve sat opposite him. Steve said nothing about the night before, so Greg kept quiet too. But he wondered if Steve had said anything to Esther.

The toast helped, but Greg felt very unsettled about what had happened. Had it really happened at all? He needed time and space to make sense of it all.

After breakfast, the four kids from Trenchard House walked to the football summer school together.

Greg said nothing. Jatinder looked across at him and was quiet too. Maddie and Jess made up for it, squabbling and bickering about nothing at all.

They got on Greg's nerves with their nonsense. What was it with them? He tried to block them out as he worked out what he'd say to Hafeez that morning.

As he walked alongside Jatinder, Greg heard an engine roar above. He looked up and saw the shadow of a plane amid the clouds.

"Why are you smiling?" Jatinder asked him.

"I was just thinking about some friends of mine," Greg told him.

"Right," Jatinder said, and gave Greg a funny look.

Greg kept smiling. He was thinking of Nokes and the other airmen. He wondered if they could see him now – down here in the 21st century?

'If they can,' he thought, 'they'll see I'm no quitter. But they know that already.'

*

Everyone was changed into their kit and Greg had on the keeper's jersey he'd worn the day before. It didn't feel like yesterday – more like a hundred yesterdays ago.

As they warmed up, Hafeez strode up to Greg.

"Nice jersey," he said. "You're a keeper today then?"

"I am."

"Meaning?"

"I want to try again."

"I see." Hafeez was smiling, but his arms were crossed over his chest. "How come?"

"What you said – and what a friend said."

"What did I say?" Hafeez asked.

"That you thought I had some talent as a keeper."

"You do," Hafeez said. "If you can focus on your position on the pitch. And what did your friend say?"

"That what he liked about me was that I never give up," Greg said.

"OK," Hafeez said. "Get in that goal then."

Greg nodded. Then he looked Hafeez in the eye and held out his hand. Hafeez smiled – a proper, broad grin – and clasped Greg's hand and shook it. Greg grinned back, then turned and jogged towards the open goal that he would make his own for the match. As he did so, Greg couldn't help but feel that Nokes would be proud of him.

ABOUT SPITFIRE

When my daughter was 8, we made an Airfix model of a Spitfire together. I used to enjoy making Airfix models when I was young and I wanted to see if she'd enjoy it too.

As we assembled and painted the model, I told her about the Spitfire pilots of the Second World War. How thousands of brave young men flew into the skies to fight against the forces of Nazi Germany, to stop them invading Britain like they had the countries of mainland Europe.

A lot of what I told my daughter, I'd learned from watching war films when I was about her age. I used to love watching them on TV on a Saturday afternoon with my grandpa, who was also called Tom.

I told her that many of the Spitfire pilots were still teenagers, barely ten years older than she was then. And when those pilots shot down German bombers, they did so to save lives at home in Britain and in Europe. This meant they took lives too – the lives of the young men in the German planes.

I told my daughter that thousands of airmen died in those battles in the sky. And not just British-born airmen. Men from Australia, New Zealand, Canada and other countries also piloted Spitfires. In particular, Polish Spitfire pilots played a vital role in stopping the German invasion of Britain. The Polish airmen were exceptional pilots, but many lost their lives flying for the RAF. Later, the Polish War Memorial near RAF Northolt was erected to remember them. This important piece of history is why I wanted Greg to be a British boy, whose parents are originally from Poland.

If Spitfire pilots were shot down but survived, they were often captured and kept as prisoners of war. In prison camps, they would be away from their loved ones for months or years, often with their family not knowing if they were dead or alive. Imagine being trapped in a prison camp with no contact with your family and friends at home.

What would you want to do?

Escape.

And that's what many of the prisoners did. They tried to escape by hiding in trucks, breaking through fences or digging tunnels. They were soldiers fighting in a war and so they saw it as their duty to escape.

When I was writing *Spitfire* I visited the RAF Museums at Cosford and Hendon to imagine what life was like during the Second World War. There are real Spitfires from the war on display, as well as the uniforms and flying gear that pilots would need to fly these planes. There are smaller items, too, like the silk maps the pilots had in case they were shot down.

These excellent displays helped me to check the facts of my story. When I saw the details of the Second World War close-up, I was inspired to bring my characters to life.

I made the character of Greg up for this book, but there was a real man called Tom Nokes. He wasn't in the RAF, but he was in the Army and, after the war, he was a policeman near Harrogate. He was my grandpa. And when I used to go round to his flat when I was young, we used to watch TV together – always either football or war films. And so I remember him, Tom Nokes, in this book.

ACKNOWLEDGEMENTS

I am always glad of all the different help I'm given in writing my books. First, help from my wife and daughter, then from my writing group – James, Anna and Ali. The pupils at three schools helped by reading the first drafts of *Spitfire*. They were Baines Endowed School in Lancashire, Albrighton Primary near RAF Cosford and All Saints Primary in Halifax. Isaac Hewson-Betts, Jim Sells and the wonderful RAF Museums (especially Phil and Al) also helped me no end. Thank you, all of you.

Thanks, too, to Emma Baker, my editor, and everyone at Barrington Stoke, a very fine publisher that I am proud to be published by.